Sundogs

Journey to the
Great Windmill

For all my dogs: We've loved each other well.

Author and illustrator photos on back cover taken by Barb Kelly.

ISBN: 978-1-59298-416-9

Library of Congress Catalog Number: 2012900500

Book design and typesetting: Jill Blumer

Printed in the United States of America

First Printing: 2012

16   15   14   13   12   5   4   3   2   1

BEAVER'S POND
PRESS

7108 Ohms Lane
Edina, Minnesota 55439 USA
(952) 829-8818
beaverspondpress.com

To order, visit BeaversPondBooks.com or call
1-800-901-3480. Reseller and special sales discounts available.

Sundogs

Journey to the
Great Windmill

Words: Kay Elliott

Pictures: Barb Björnson

BEAVER'S
POND
PRESS

As Mom tucked Kady into bed, SuSu was curled up at Kady's side as usual. Every night, Kady petted SuSu's soft fur until she fell asleep.

SuSu was a gray dog, but tonight, as Kady looked close, she noticed that SuSu had different shades of red mixed into her dark fur.

"Look, Mom, SuSu is a red dog!" said Kady. At first Mom was puzzled, but then she looked closer and saw SuSu's red fur.

"You're right, Kady!" said Mom.

"Mom, where did SuSu's red come from?" Kady asked.

"Hmmm. . . ." said Mom. "Remember when we picked SuSu? We felt like she was choosing us?"

"Oh, yes!" said Kady. It was time for one of Mom's stories!

Mom began. . . .

Millions of miles away from Earth, close to the sun, there is a bright and colorful world called Planet of the Sundogs. All dogs live on this planet before they come to their Earth families.

SuSu was a very curious and brave sundog. Her fur was the most beautiful shade of red. Even though her curiosity led her to fun and excitement, she still felt that something was missing from her life.

One day, SuSu found herself in trouble from her latest adventure. As she struggled to get free, another sundog happened by. His fur was a calming blue color. She called out, "Hello down there! Would you take a moment to help me down? I am getting a bit uncomfortable!"

"I can surely help you! My name is Yogi." Yogi, a smart and sensible sundog, chewed away the vines and freed SuSu.

"Thank you so much, Yogi! Where are you heading?" SuSu asked.

"I'm looking for a home," Yogi replied. "I want a place not just to live, but also to feel safe and loved."

SuSu said, "I think we would make a good team. Let's travel together to find this place called home. I am never afraid to try new things, and you will keep us safe." Yogi agreed, and together they set out to follow where the sun led them.

As Yogi and SuSu followed the sun, they found themselves on a mountain path. Looking up, they noticed a bright orange glow off in the distance. When they got close, they found that it was a determined little sundog pulling on a blanket stuck under a big rock.

"What are you doing, little sundog?" Yogi asked.

"ARRRRRRRRRGGGGGGGHHHHHHH!!" the sundog cried as he yanked on the blanket. "My blanket is stuck!" He stopped pulling with a sigh. "My name is Harley. Who are you?"

"I'm SuSu, and this is Yogi. Let us help!" offered SuSu. Harley looked like he didn't trust them at first, but there was no other way to get his prized possession back. Working together, the three sundogs freed the blanket.

After thanking them, Harley inquired, "How did you find me way up here?"

Yogi answered, "We saw your orange glow and had to investigate!"

Harley shared, "I've been all alone since I was born. My blanket is all I have." He was such a sweet, lovable sundog that SuSu and Yogi invited him to join their search.

Day after day, the three sundogs followed the sun. SuSu led them with bravery. Now that Harley was with them, Yogi was even more protective of his young friends. Harley was determined to keep up with the bigger sundogs, so he ran as hard as his short legs could take him!

One evening, after a particularly busy and fun day, the sundogs found themselves dirty, hungry, and oh so tired. Suddenly, they sniffed a scent so delicious it made them drool! They followed their noses to a cozy cottage. As they approached, a most beautiful sundog with rich purple fur came outside.

"Welcome, my sundog friends!" said the purple sundog. "My name is Bo. Oh dear, you all look like you could use a meal and a bath!"

"We surely could!" yawned SuSu.

Bo said, "I have a nice warm pool here for your baths, and after that you can share my dinner." Soon the sundogs were clean and dry and enjoying a home-cooked meal. After dinner, Bo said, "It's too late for you to walk any further. Why don't you rest here for the night?"

As Bo tucked them into bed, Harley asked, "Have we found our home?" Yogi and SuSu's ears perked up, because they had been wondering the same thing.

Bo answered gently, "No, this isn't your home. I have made this a most comfortable place, but I sense there is more to a real home. Let me tell you a bedtime story, one that my sundog grandma told me long ago." The sundogs eagerly listened.

"When we have become the very best sundogs we can be, we find a special place called the Great Windmill. The Great Windmill is the brightest and most colorful place on the sundog planet. When sundogs find it, a magical thing happens! They are so overcome with happiness that they float away to a place called Earth, where they find home. When they get there, they feel only love forever after. My grandma found that windmill, and though I didn't see her again, we heard she looked so happy when she left the planet!"

That night, the four sundogs all dreamed about the Great Windmill. Each one of them dreamed about home, but every sundog's dream was different.

When they woke up the next morning, Harley, Yogi, and SuSu begged Bo to come along on their search for home. Bo knew she must leave her warm cottage if she was ever going to find her real home. As they trotted off, SuSu smiled as she thought, "Bo is just like a mother to us." They were becoming a sundog family!

The sundogs continued on, always following the sun. One day they came to a beautiful park. From up on the hill, Yogi could see a crowd gathering around an unusual green glow.

At the bottom of the hill, the travelers found a green sundog who was telling stories and performing tricks. "I am Zeke, and I hope you are enjoying my show!" they heard him say. All around him, sundogs were laughing and enjoying themselves.

The travelers waited as he finished his last silly tale and introduced themselves. Then Bo asked, "May we please pet you?"

Zeke chuckled and nodded, and the other four sundogs stroked the thickest, softest fur they had ever felt. Zeke replied, "For some reason, anyone who pets me feels better!"

As Zeke rose stiffly to stand they saw he was the biggest, most magnificent sundog they had ever seen. However, it was plain that he wasn't standing quite right. Harley asked, "What happened to your legs?"

"Well, I was born with bad legs," Zeke explained, "but the sundoctors fixed me up. Now I do quite well, thank you! I don't really even notice anymore."

The sundogs told Zeke of their journey to find a home. Zeke said, "A real home often shows up in my dreams, too." But when the sundogs asked him to join them, he said, "I fear I would slow you down too much."

"Oh, no!" Bo said, "A slower pace could make our trip even more fun, especially with a one-of-a-kind sundog like you along!"

Many days and many adventures later . . .

The sundogs were preparing their favorite evening meal. They noticed a bright yellow glow moving here and there in the forest. Suddenly a ball bounced into their circle. As Zeke caught it, the others looked around and spotted an adorable, sparkly yellow puppy nosing out of the woods.

The little sundog's name was Juno. Juno was shy, but she loved to play! She could not take her eyes off the ball as Zeke bounced it.

Juno timidly asked, "Would you play catch with me?" Zeke threw the ball as far as he could, and Juno sprang into action.

That night, Juno joined them for dinner. "These are the best hot dogs and dog biscuits I have ever tasted!" she said. After their meal, the sundogs relaxed around the campfire and told stories.

"Tell us your story, Juno," SuSu said.

Juno had been listening to the others, but hadn't said much herself. She cleared her throat.

"Well I am very young, so there is not much to tell," she began. "My litter was born in the shadow of a big, beautiful windmill. I was playing one day and got lost. All I want to do is go home, back to the windmill. It felt so wonderful there!"

The sundogs wagged their tails in excitement over Juno's memory of her home. Could this be the same windmill they were searching for? Yogi suggested, "As we follow the sun, let's keep our eyes out for Juno's windmill." They were happy to invite Juno, the playful puppy, to join their growing family. And then they played!

One day as they traveled, the sundogs saw lights bursting through the sky—on and off, on and off. They followed the sun, and they found it low in the sky behind a huge machine with six turning arms.

"That is my windmill!" shouted Juno as she raced toward it. The other sundogs followed slowly, awed by the slow turning of the arms. They had found the Great Windmill!

The six sundogs gathered together at the base of the windmill. As each arm of the Great Windmill came around it swept up one of the sundogs, until they were all spinning together in a whirlwind. As they barked with delight, all of their colors mixed together, making the most beautiful rainbow of hues.

Then they began drifting farther and farther into the sky, away from the Great Windmill and away from the Planet of the Sundogs.

As they glided through space, their planet got smaller and smaller and smaller. Soon, they were so far away that they couldn't see the Planet of the Sundogs anymore!

But then they felt themselves being pulled gently toward a beautiful planet glowing with greens and blues. "This must be Earth!" they barked to one another. They were heading HOME!

Mom noticed Kady's sleepy eyes and ended softly, "Be sure to look up to the sky whenever you are outside. Someday you will be lucky enough to see a sundog. The sundogs play in the sunlight, waiting patiently for their Earth families to call them home. When a family wishes for a special dog of their very own, the sundogs come down to love and be loved beyond their wildest sundog dreams!"

Just as all people are different, all dogs are, too. There are black ones, brown ones, and white ones with spots, in all different shapes and sizes. Look more closely at the special dogs in your life. Can you see their sundog colors?

These and other dogs available for adoption and fostering at PetProjectRescue.com.

Photographs by Megan Bluma.